JEANETTE WINTER

The Christmas Tree Ship

PHILOMEL BOOKS • NEW YORK

Philomel Books, a division of The Putnam & Grosset Group,
200 Madison Avenue, New York, NY 10016. Philomel Books, Reg. U.S. Pat. & Tm. Off.
Published simultaneously in Canada. Printed in Hong Kong by South China Printing Co. (1988) Ltd.
Book design by Gunta Alexander. The text is set in Administer.
Library of Congress Cataloging-in-Publication Data
Winter, Jeanette. The Christmas Tree Ship / written and illustrated by Jeanette Winter.
p.   cm.   Summary: Each winter Captain Herman fills his fishing schooner with Christmas trees,
sails down Lake Michigan, and delivers the trees to the residents of Chicago.
[1. Christmas trees—Fiction.   2. Christmas—Fiction.   3. Ships—Fiction.]   I. Title.
PZ7.W7547Ch   1994   [E]—dc20   93-36341   CIP   AC   ISBN 0-399-22693-1
1   3   5   7   9   10   8   6   4   2
First Impression

for Ruthie and Jim

The Christmas Tree Ship is based on a true story. In the winter of 1887, eighteen-year-old Herman Schuenemann first loaded his fishing schooner, the *Rouse Simmons*, with spruce trees from Manistique, Michigan, and sailed down Lake Michigan to Chicago, bringing the trees in time for Christmas. He brought trees to the city every year. During a winter storm in 1912, the *Rouse Simmons* was lost at sea. Captain Schuenemann's widow and three daughters carried on the tradition after the tragedy, bringing a ship filled with trees down to Chicago for twenty-two more years.

Chop, chop, chop went the axes, cutting down spruce trees in the wintry northern woods. Each year on the last day in November, Captain Herman and his crew cut trees to bring to the city in time for Christmas.

The captain's wife, Hannah, and their girls, Hazel and
Pearl and little Elsie, were there every year, helping.

In summer the captain's ship was a fishing schooner, but every winter it became the *Christmas Tree Ship*. Captain Herman loaded it with trees and sailed down Lake Michigan to the city of Chicago, where everyone knew him.

Hannah and the girls watched and waved good-bye on
a frosty morning.

Friendly gulls stayed close as the *Christmas Tree Ship*
made its way down the icy waters of the winter lake.

Night fell, snowflakes fell, like stars falling all around.
Night on the lake was the captain's favorite time.

The quiet of the lake gave way to the hustle and bustle
of the city, as the ship made its way up the Chicago River
to the Clark Street Bridge.

Old friends and new customers greeted the captain,
and asked about Hannah and their little daughters.
Captain Herman had many friends.

Fathers and sons carried trees home through snow covered streets.

Warm lights in bright rooms beckoned everyone home.

Spruce trees from far, far away stood gaily decorated
in cozy houses all through the city.

Back home in the quiet north, Hannah and Hazel and Pearl and Elsie watched the lake for the captain's return, as they did every year.

The next year it snowed and snowed as the captain cut trees for the city.

He hugged his family good-bye before he sailed off
into the stormy waters, loaded down with the trees.

Heavy snow became a blizzard that raged on the land
and the lake.

Soon the *Christmas Tree Ship* was almost invisible as
the snow and wind howled around her.

The captain and his crew struggled against the storm. Trees flew into the dark water. The little lifeboat came loose and disappeared into the whiteness.

Tearing a page from the ship's log, Captain Herman
wrote a message to his family. He sealed it in a bottle
and threw it overboard.

When the storm cleared, mothers and fathers and sons
and daughters waited on the Clark Street Bridge for the
Christmas Tree Ship.

The newspapers reported that the captain was missing. From sunrise to sunset ships of all kinds searched and searched in the icy waters.

Then two fishermen found spruce trees caught up in their nets. But the *Christmas Tree Ship* never arrived in the city.

A bottle washed up on the Wisconsin shore a few days
later. Inside was Captain Herman's message. It said:
My dear Hannah and dear daughters,
The storm is bad—we are struggling.
I send my love to you. —Herman

Hannah waited and waited for word from Herman.
But the message never reached her.
Hannah grieved for her husband.
Hazel and Pearl and Elsie missed their dear father.

But when the snows of November blew in again,
Hannah knew what she must do.

She hired a crew and guided the cutting of the trees. And Hazel and Pearl and Elsie helped their mother to carry on their father's work.

A new schooner was loaded down with spruces. Hannah and the girls and women from the town sailed with the crew down the lake to the city. All the way there they wove garlands and wreaths and sang carols.

From the Clark Street Bridge, the captain's old
customers saw a ship in the distance, all aglow with
candlelight and filled with trees. Word soon spread that
the *Christmas Tree Ship* was on its way.

Everyone was there to welcome Hannah and her girls
as the new ship sailed into the river. As young and old
alike joined in the singing, the city was filled with the
sounds and lights of Christmas once again.

And for many, many more years, the *Christmas Tree Ship* brought trees down the lake to the city, just in time for Christmas.